For Gillian, on her birthday
July 14, 2008

These other strange sto
task of the culture we might have missed.
Let's make up for it next time we're in
Africa!

May the laughter never be far from your cheeks.

xox Luc

THE RAIN BULL

Eugène Marais's dwaalstories in Afrikaans first appeared in the magazine *Die Boerevrou* in 1921, and was subsequently published in book form by Nasionale Pers in 1927. Human & Rousseau first published *Dwaalstories* in 1959 with line drawings by Katrine Harries, and that edition was reprinted regularly, until the second edition was published in 2006.

THE RAIN BULL
and Other Tales from the San
Eugène N. Marais

Translated by
JACQUES COETZEE

Illustrations by
KATRINE HARRIES

HUMAN & ROUSSEAU

Cape Town Pretoria

The author's original notes are numbered, and the words marked with an
asterisk are explained in the translator's glossary

Translator's acknowledgements:
My thanks to Annie Gagiano, whose work on Marais first inspired this translation.
A special word of thanks is also due to Marie Louise Rousseau for hours of often
passionate debate over countless details of the manuscript
during its early stages.

Copyright in translation © 2007 by Jacques Coetzee
First published in 2007 by Human & Rousseau,
a division of NB Publishers (Pty) Limited,
40 Heerengracht, Cape Town, 8001 (Head office)
Cover design and typography by Chérie Collins
Set in 11.5 on 17 pt Bembo
Printed and bound by Paarl Print, Oosterland Street, Paarl, South Africa

ISBN-10 0-7981-4833-0
ISBN-13 978-0-7981-4833-7

All rights reserved
No part of this book may be reproduced or transmitted in any form or by
any electronic or mechanical means, including photocopying and
recording, or by any other information storage or retrieval system,
without written permission from the publisher

INTRODUCTION

THE LEARNED GERMAN, Dr Bleek, who studied the Bushman language and literature in the Cape about fifty years ago – a literature without letters! – and made a large collection of Bushman tales and poems for the Cape Library, tells how his investigation was made difficult by a surprising discovery he made early on. He found that in the animal stories each animal spoke its own, distinct language! The lion had its own language, which was quite different from that spoken by the jackal. Someone who wanted to tell the animal stories therefore had to learn ten or twelve different languages or dialects. How far the animal languages differed from the actual Bushman language and from one another, I cannot say; but the effect of the languages on the later Afrikaans Bushman tales was peculiar. Most original Bushman tales contain numerous songs and poems spoken by some animal or another. Now, when the Bushman language itself was dying out, the narrators translated the stories into their own peculiar Afrikaans. Some of the animal songs and poems remained in existence even after the narrators no longer remembered their meaning. In due course they became a mixture of Bushman and Afrikaans, utterly meaningless. Sound was the important thing, meaning a secondary affair. Out of this the so-called "dwaalstorie" *(wandering tale) doubtlessly came into being. Some of the stories are merely a sequence of words with a faint shadow of meaning. In others again the meaning is clearer. And this latter kind reminds one of the earliest European children's songs and poems that have survived through the ages; also mere words and rhymes with a very obscure meaning.

The Bushmen's "dwaalstories" always had a great attraction for Afrikaans children. The writer knows an Afrikaans family Grobler, who had an old Bushman, Outa Flip, in their service. All the children grew up more or less under his supervision. He was a famous storyteller. He knew the "Jakkals en Wolf" saga from A to Z, and wandering tales without end. The children always chose a wandering tale when the choice was left to them, and even today they can recite a multitude of them, word for word, and Outa Flip has been in his grave these thirty years! Some of the so-called stories are in pure rhyme. This must, of course, be attributed to the white man's influence. The original Bushmen knew nothing of rhyme. Others again contain so much meaning that it is clear that the sequence of words originally told a real story.

For years the writer himself knew an old Bushman, Outa Hendrik. He was more than a hundred years old when he died some years ago. Erich Mayer made a painting of the old man shortly before his death. Old Hendrik could also recite a number of wandering tales, which was interesting to the writer because these tales attached much more value to meaning than the Grobler type mentioned above. All the stories contained at least the suggestion of a sequence of narrative events – just enough to move the lively imagination of a child powerfully. Someone who is interested in the psychology of children will soon realise where the attraction of the story lies.

I should like to attempt a rendering of a few of old Hendrik's wandering tales. Unfortunately I did not write down any of them word for word. I wrote down a few immediately after the telling. I regret to admit that much has been lost. The peculiar Afrikaans-Bushman words and expressions have mostly escaped me, and the suitable gestures, natural imitations and expressions cannot be rendered in writing. The reader has perhaps had the personal experience and possesses the necessary imaginative powers to add them himself.

E.N.M.
1927

LITTLE REED-ALONE-IN-THE-WHIRLPOOL

The first message bearer at Grammadoekies was the little yellow Bushman Reed-alone-in-the-Whirlpool.

His ta's ta,* old Heitsi-eibib, gave him the name when

he was still sitting in the carrying-skin. He could run so fast that the dust whirled underneath his heels; and when he gave his all, he became just a tiny dot in the middle of the track.

And then the great danger came to Grammadoekies. Old Heitsi-eibib called a council in the night, for the need was pressing. He even sent for old Klipdas-One-eye to sit with them, and he was so old that his jaw was worn away and his eyes were so shrivelled that they were almost closed. All night they sat round the fire by the tgorra,[1] and it was old Klipdas-One-eye who put together the big word. And with the dawn they called Reed-alone to carry the message to Red Joggom.

And when he came, he heard the old women in the reed huts shouting: "Hot-Tgorra! Hot-Tgorra!" And the men were so afraid that their toenails clattered and the sweat poured from their bodies like hailstones. Each of them could blow out the fire with a single breath.

And when the day grew white, he set off from Grammadoekies. He carried a string instrument in his left hand and with his right fist he beat his forehead; for every word of the message a blow with the fist – so that he would not forget.

The last words of his Old Ta had been: "Beware of Nagali: She will waylay you in many ways; she has strong magic. If you do wrong, your body will be stretched as tight as the string of the great ramkie!"*

When the sun was high, they could still see the little whirlwinds twisting underneath his feet on the last ridge, but Reed-alone himself was just a dot on the track.

Then Klipdas-One-eye said: "Arrie! The sparks are in the wolf's tail." For it was he who had put together the big word.

And when Reed could no longer see his own shadow, he looked at the track ahead, and there he saw a lean Bushman girl. She trod a few slow dance steps across the track. "Arrie, girl," Reed said, "can you dance?"

"My brother!" she said. "What do you place on the anthill?"

"It's the best string instrument," said Reed, and he placed it on the anthill. "And what does my girl have?"

She took the string of blue beads from her neck and put it down. And then they set off across the veld. As far as the third anthill they stayed together, and then the girl started dancing rings around him, and in a wide half-moon she turned back to Grammadoekies. And Reed wanted to shout: "This way, my girl! This way!" But his breath was small, and she danced so fast that she blew the words away from his mouth. And Reed's heart grew small, and he thought: "I will run as hard as I can and save my instrument." But as he started off, he saw the dark girl dancing far ahead of him like a floating cloud on the mountain top; and he was still far away when she grabbed the instrument and hung her beads around her neck. And he heard her laughing, and she called: "My boy, my fireplace is up above. I will give Nagali your regards." And as she danced away, he saw that it was really the whirlwind of the great desert.

And then he said: "Hot-Tgorra! The string of the great ramkie!" for the sun was going down and Red Joggom was far!

And he set off again, but he no longer repeated the

message, for the sorrow of the string instrument was in his heart.

And he ate the track as far as the neck of the midmost mountain. Then he saw a Bushman sitting beside the loose stone to the left of the track, and as he ran he heard the grey fellow calling: "What is the sadness that makes my brother walk so slowly today?"

And Reed-alone stopped next to him. "Can my brother run?" he asked.

"The girls of Jakkalsdraai* have told me so," said the grey Bushman.

And Reed's heart burned in him, for he had not yet found anyone who could breathe his dust.

"Shall it be to the top of the neck?" asked Reed-alone.

"Heitse!" the grey Bushman said. "The baboon runs up the mountain. No, my brother, it shall be to the sharp stone," and he pointed back down the hollow, and they made ready. And when they set off, the grey Bushman slipped away from Reed. And Reed closed his eyes tightly, and gave his all. And when he felt the ground level under his feet, he looked again, and he saw the grey Bushman like a small dust cloud far ahead on the track. And when he put his hand over his eyes, he saw that it was Nagali's little oribi.* And he clapped his hand over his mouth, and his heart grew soft in his body. And he turned around and leaped up the mountain, and only said: "My ta's ta!"

It was dark when Reed-alone reached the bank of Moetmekaar's Drift: and there he stopped for the first time. When the lightning flashed, he said: "Heitse! It's Nagali making light to look for me!" and he put his body out of sight.

In the distance he could hear the black water rumbling, for the river was angry, and in the drift in front of him he saw the evening light flash in the water of the whirlpool like the tail of a fish.

"It's going through or it's the string of the ramkie!" said Reed-alone, and he stepped into the water.

And on the other side, against the bank, sat old Nagali's Narra stick, and Reed-alone heard her laughing at him. And then he said: "Heitse! Soon we will talk to each other face to face. My fireplace is up above!" And there and then the great misfortune befell him. He forgot that they had heard at Grammadoekies that Nagali had at last found the magic wand that made her mistress of the crocodile.

And as Reed-alone walked into the black water and felt it churn, he sang the magic song:

> I'll grab one side and you'll grab the other,
> All you yellow things, grab one another.

But it was no use. He saw the whirlpool ahead of him close to the opposite bank, and going through was impossible. And then he saw right next to him the huge mimosa stump with one end in the shallow water. He climbed up slowly and glanced at where Nagali's Narra stick sat and he laughed out loud in the hollow of his hand. And then he felt the mimosa stump move under him, and move under him, and he held on with all his nails, and he called his great-grandfather's great name, three times. But it was no use.

He heard the Narra stick calling: "My boy, where is your fireplace?"

But he had forgotten the answer.

Then he saw that it was Nagali's crocodile; and when he came to, he was lying high on the sandy bank from which he had set out; but he did not know this.

And he set off and once again began to beat his forehead, and he remembered Heitsi-eibib's message again, and he dashed off into the night. And in front of him he saw the great fire, and he stopped among them just as the day dawned red, and he started reciting his message. But before he was halfway, they seized him, and then he saw that he was back at Grammadoekies, and that it was his own grandfather who had him by the left leg.

And Heitsi-eibib said to old Klipdas-One-eye: "We must stretch him tighter than the string of the great ramkie!"

And there they put out the fire of Reed-alone-in-the-Whirlpool.

THE SONG OF THE RAIN
A Koranna Wandering Tale

IT WAS THE TIME when Hunchback Joggom Konterdans of Das-se-Kant* made the first violin with four strings; it was when old Jakob Makding* made himself Strongman of the Berry Trees. He dug trenches with snares all round, and laid poisoned darts in the tracks, and closed off the Slow Water with hook-thorn twigs; and all day long he strutted around the werf,* and at night and at dawn he blew the great horn. And his little ones at the edge of the werf jeered at the people passing by.

"A-we!" they said. "The grey baboons dig for roots in the hard earth, and at dawn they suck the morning's water from the grass blades."

And it was a great disgrace.

And no-one from Das-se-Kant, or from the other places was allowed to go near the water; and those who went near the shade of the Trees had to say the sweet word and sprinkle buchu under the arms of Jakob Makding.[2]

And the rain stayed away, and the rain stayed away.

And everyone outside the place of the Berry Trees was pale, for the fat was used up and the hunger great. They searched for roots into the night, and sucking water[3] was all that was left.

And when the rain had stayed away for a long time, Tuit-Miershoop,* the headman of Das-se-Kant, called together the Great Council. And Hunchback Joggom Konterdans worked at his violin. He had heard the elders by the fire tell that the Master Makers of old turned fine strings from sinews of the white-backed badger; and that each was rubbed for a month with eland's root until every thread was a spider web.

And the thornwood that grows in the stony crevices was rubbed with white sandstone until it hummed in the wind, and then the holes were burned over a fire of tamboti wood, and this was the violin of the Master Makers who trekked through the Great River with Jonkman Afrikaner. And Little Joggom Konterdans took the badger sinews, and searched long in the mountains; and in the evening, when the little ones dug for uintjies,* he fetched eland's roots from the sandy flats; and he twisted and stretched the strings until they looked like threaded hail; and at night on the sleeping-mat he rubbed the wooden frame until it roared like the wind in the great cavern.

And the rain stayed away.

And the Strong Council came together in the werf of Das-se-Kant, and everyone complained about Makding and the Berry Trees, and told of the Slow Water and the abundant food. And the old woman Nasi-Tgam took the word:

"When I go near the Berry Trees in the hollow of the night, I hear people walking below the wind. It is the dead of Heitsi-eibib who made the Law of the Berry Trees: The Strongman is chosen and the Strongman must stand guard; but when the rain stays away and the great hunger comes, then the food and water must be shared. Ai! Where are the hunters of old, and the man who can make the great song? Where is the warrior who grabs the grey Lion by the tail and says: 'Brother, I am here?' Where the Master Songmaker? For I hear tell that the One at the Berry Trees speaks great words that there are no other players on this side of the river. Jakob Makding grew up among his people, and he could make many songs, and there was no-one who could play along with him. And he was a great hunter. Ai! Our hunters! When Pylstert* coughs, they fight the dassies for a hiding-place in the crevices. And the dead who walk below the wind at night say that if the man comes, the best songmaker, Jakob Makding will go limp without a single blow. Winter will come over him; his leaves will fall."

And then Tonteldoos Vuurdop,* master of the Wienslig werf, took the word. (When it came to talking, he was never far away.) And he said to the old woman Nasi-Tgam: "Of grabbing the lion's tail I cannot speak, for the Man has many followers and defences, and they speak also of a sharp knife. But when it comes to playing and the making of songs, then your Brother from Wienslig is still here. Where is the whirring stick, and the song of the Quagga that he made of old? When he blows at Wienslig by night, the male lions answer, down by the Berry Pan, where the bushes grow small."

Then the old woman Nasi-Tgam said: "My Brother from Wienslig has spoken the words. It is he who will blow tonight at the Berry Trees, inside the boundary of the werf. It is he who will give us back the water."

And everyone said it was the true word, and they said sweet things about Tonteldoos Vuurdop; and Tuit-Miershoop of Das-se-Kant called him his brother-in-law. But Tonteldoos would not meet the eyes of the old woman Nasi-Tgam.

And while the Council was talking inside, Hunchback Joggom Konterdans made a small fire of tamboti twigs behind the goat pen; and for the last time he smoothed his strings with the fresh juice of eland's root, until they looked like the rain shooting through the firelight; and he coloured the wooden frame in the tamboti smoke, and he stretched his bow made of a quagga's tail, and he tightened his strings and fastened the ears, and softly stroked the strings with the bow.

And all those in the Tgorra listened. And Tonteldoos said: "Why do we keep council and talk of making songs? Here comes the rain!"

And then the little ones laughed outside: "Narri! Not a single thunderclap! It's Joggom Konterdans making his violin." But when they came out, the fire was dead and he had gone.

And that night at Das-se-Kant they listened for the whirring stick of Tonteldoos from the direction of the Berry Trees. And the old woman Nasi-Tgam sang the song of the Garden Nightshade who disappeared when it was his turn to stand guard at the tiger hole. And when the dawn came, they heard Lion Makding blow his horn down in the place of the Berry Trees.

Then Tuit-Miershoop said: "Now I know! My old brother-in-law Tonteldoos has died!" And they ran to Wienslig to bring the sad word to his family. And when they came there, they saw Tonteldoos sitting in the sun in the corner of the shelter, and he was rubbing his legs with leguaan fat. And he sighed deeply. Then Tuit-Miershoop said: "Now I know! The prop and stay of our house is broken! The eggshell of my brother's whirring stick is broken!" And Tonteldoos sighed again. And he said: "My old brother, to tell you the actual truth, the eggshell is whole and the whirring stick still in use – but to tell you the real truth, it's my old uncle – you all know my old uncle has long been hanging between life and death; and when I had prepared everything in the darkness, my old uncle suddenly got the black cramp in his stomach. I saw it was a great sickness, and the master medicine is scarce; my heart yearns for Jakob Makding, but who can leave his closest family alone in the night with a great sickness? Now good health has been restored to the shelter." And everyone said that it was the true word.

And the old woman Nasi-Tgam sang softly: "Ai! The black cramp! The black cramp!" And Tonteldoos Vuurdop would not meet her eyes.

This was the time that one of the little ones of the fat woman from Putkuil swallowed the arrowhead, and she invited all the people to come and weep. It was the greatest weeping of that drought. They cut up the lean sheep that had been caught by the jackal, and each one was given a piece of tail fat. And Short Little Joggom Konterdans walked through the home veld to look for uintjies, and his violin was in his hand.

And when the elders were weeping in front of the reed hut, the little ones shouted: "Something is coming! It sounds like a snake in the dry grass." And they heard the playing of the violin, and they started with their feet, and the elders stood up, and they said: "Arrie! Is there a wedding in the land?" And when he came up to them, they were all stamping their feet.

And inside the little one lay dead from the arrowhead.

And the old woman Nasi-Tgam went to meet him, and she waved the big black kaross, and she went to meet him with a calabash of sour porridge and a handful of tail fat. And from afar she said: "Heitse! The Little Hunchback! The Little Yellow Baboon who looks behind him and makes the tiger stop in his tracks! He it is who will show Makding the way out of here and save the Berry Trees!" And she gave him the little mirror of polished rhinoceros horn that she had made long ago; and also the great copper neck ring of Heitsi-eibib.

And that morning at the breaking of the day Konterdans sat on the Pointed Stone inside the werf of the Berry Trees; it is at the edge of the Slow Water; and he turned his back to the shelters. And in front of him lay the rhinoceros mirror of Nasi-Tgam, so that he could see everything behind him; and he had rubbed himself with tail fat so that he glistened. And around his head hung three meerkat* skins; and around his neck was the great copper ring of Heitsi-eibib.

And he made the Song of the Rain.

And Jakob Makding, when he took his horn and

opened his mouth to blow, stood just so. And his little ones rushed from the direction of the shelter and they shouted: "Our Ta, our Ta, there is someone on the beacon stone near the Slow Water who shows only his back. And the people are dancing in the shelters."

And Jakob Makding grabbed his knife, and he called to the warriors, but there was no answer. He heard them say: "Klips! But that is the master player, that one."

And Makding beat the great drum, and he called: "Today I invite all the vultures! Today will be the great battle of the Berry Trees!" And he crept up on Konterdans from behind the thorn shelter at the Slow Water.

And Konterdans sang the Song of the Rain, and he played his violin.

And Makding saw his own people going out to meet him, and they danced and spoke sweet words to Joggom Konterdans. And on the ridge he saw the old woman Nasi-Tgam and she spread the black kaross wide, and behind her came the people from all the other places, with calabashes and eggshells ready for the water, and he felt his heart grow weak.

And Hunchback Joggom Konterdans played the Song of the Rain, and he spied him in the mirror.

And then Jakob Makding threw his knife into the Slow Water, and sat down in the dust, and he called out: "My little ones, my little ones, your Ta's horse has died!"

And that day the old woman Nasi-Tgam told them about the Law of the Berry Trees again, and it was Hunchback Joggom Konterdans who handed out the water.

THE SONG OF THE RAIN
(Of Hunchback Joggom Konterdans)

First over the mountain top she looks shyly,
And her eyes are bashful;
And she laughs softly.
And from afar she beckons with one hand.
Her bracelets shine and her beads shimmer;
Softly she calls.
She tells the winds about the dance.
And she invites them, for the way is wide and the
wedding-feast abundant.

The big game rush in from the plains.
They gather on the ridges.
Wide flare their nostrils,
And they swallow the wind;
And they bend low, to see her fine tracks in the sand.

The small game deep under the Earth hear the
shuffling of her feet,
And they creep closer and sing softly:
"Our Sister! Our Sister! You've come! You've come!"

And her beads shake,
Till the elders on the sleeping-mats start from their
sleep in the night
And speak together in the dark;
And her copper ring shimmers in the fading of the sun.
On her forehead is the fiery plume of the mountain eagle;
She steps down from the heights;
She spreads out the grey kaross with both arms;
The wind grows out of breath.

O, the dance of our Sister!

THE LITTLE GREY PIPIT

THE LITTLE GIRL Nampti, the little grey pipit, was so small that the hand-reared kids could push her over in their play.

The grandmother was so old that she could barely

gather wood every day. Nampti had to make the fire, cook the food and tend the goats. And the others in the werf treated these two badly. If there was meat, they got nothing, and the young girls jeered at the grandmother because her back was bent and she was lame in one leg. They called her the Old Wolf.[4]

And on the plain Nampti found a little grey pipit's nest, and she herded the goats away from it and she sang to the mother:

> Gampta, my little grey sister!
> All that I have in the world
> Except for my old grandmother.
> When you sing up in the sky,
> You can see all the wonderful things below:
> Where the hare hides
> And the steenbok makes his shelter.
> And the women cannot touch you,
> For you are stronger than everyone,
> Although you are weaker than I.
> Even the mountain lion that frightens us

When he roars at night,
Cannot touch you.
I will look after you, my little sister,
Till all your little ones are grown.

And the little grey pipit sang overhead in the sky:

My little grey sister Nampti,
I see you![5]
I will tell you a great thing:
Last night while the Female Ostrich[6]
Was fading away with her little ones,
The mountain lion, that frightens you,
Trod on the poisoned dart in the fountain kloof,
And he lies dead in the great ghwarrie bush.
The one who pierces his skin with a lion's whisker,
Becomes a lion for as long as the Female Ostrich
Grazes in the great veld with her little ones.

And she rolled her little kaross over one arm and ran to the fountain kloof; and she saw the mountain lion that had been frightening the people for a long time lying in the ghwarrie bush. And she pulled the longest bristle from his whiskers and pushed it into the skin of her arm.

And the female pipit sang in the sky overhead: "My little grey sister Nampti! Now she is stronger than everyone; and especially the women who mock her grandmother."

And that night, when she came home with the goats, her grandmother said: "Why do the eyes shine in the dark like that?" And Nampti laughed.

And when the moon rose, she got up from the sleeping-mat and she went out. And outside the dogs were howling, and the goats were bleating behind the shelters. And she saw that her shadow was the shadow of the mountain lion. And she crept stealthily to the shelter of the Headman, Oukiep. They were sitting by the fire, cooking meat, and around them stood the calabashes of milk. And Nampti growled through the branches, and they all jumped up and ran into the reed hut and slammed the door, and inside she heard the women scream. And she took the fattest piece of meat and the biggest calabash of milk, and she carried them to her grandmother. And while they were eating, the old woman, who was blind in the dark, said: "Why does my little one lap with the tongue when she drinks milk? A person does not drink like that." And Nampti laughed out loud.

And every night she walked out when the Female Ostrich was up above, and she carried the best of the food into their shelter.

And by day the young women said: "Why is it that the Little Grey Pipit is growing so fat and big and beautiful? Where does the bent old Wolf find the food to give her?"

And Nampti just laughed.

And when she was grown, all the young men said: "There is not a single young girl among us who is Nampti's equal!"

And little Oukiep, the son of the Headman, brought ten goats to the grandmother to ask for her. And Nampti said: "If you will always take care of my Little Grey Sister as long as her nest lies in the grass, you can have me." And he promised.

And it was the biggest wedding-feast that the people had ever held.

And when the food had been apportioned, Nampti brought a fat reedbuck from her shelter. And little Oukiep said: "What kind of wife did I get? Where does a girl find the strength to catch a buck at night?"

And Nampti just laughed; but the bridegroom's heart trembled. And when Nampti was walking in the veld that day, the little pipit sang overhead in the sky:

"Nampti, my Little Grey Sister, must never drink during the night; and when she wakes suddenly, she must cover her head with the kaross."

And that night when Nampti was sleeping in the new reed hut, she woke suddenly, and she got up to drink water from the large calabash on the food shelf. And little Oukiep saw her, and he hid under the bedding.

And when it grew light, he met with the headmen and the councillors and he said: "At night her eyes glow like green fire, and she laps with the tongue when she drinks water."

And the councillors said: "This is a very bad thing. We shall stand guard tonight and peep through the smoke-hole, and if it is so, we shall rid the werf of the beast."

And behind the palings Nampti heard what they were saying.

And when the grass was almost dry, she walked in the veld and she called: "O, my Little Grey Sister, the heart of your sister is heavy. You helped me once and now, through your word, I shall come to great harm!"

And tears flowed from her eyes.

And the Little Grey Pipit sang over her head: "Where is the danger? Is it not the man's duty to rub buchu onto the arms of the woman?" And Nampti laughed as she walked back to the shelter.

And when night fell, she said: "My husband, is it not the custom that the man should rub buchu onto the bride's arms? Why then is this custom dead in our house?"

And little Oukiep took the crushed buchu out of the little skin bag and he rubbed her arms. And it grew dark; and behind the palings sat the councillors. And little Oukiep said:

"Why do my Nampti's eyes glow green in the dark?" And Nampti laughed. And again he said: "Why do my Nampti's nails grow crooked and long?" And Nampti laughed.

And his voice trembled and he said: "Why are there hairs on my Nampti's arms?" And Nampti laughed and she said: "Rub the buchu; let us keep the custom."

And his heart grew weak; and he said: "There is a thorn in my Nampti's arm."

And Nampti said: "Is it not the man's duty then to pull it out?" And he rubbed in the buchu, and he felt her arm become the front paw of the lion, and her voice grew deep. And he pulled out the whisker and he called to the councillors: "It's a lion! Help me, my Ta, or I am done for!"

And they ran in with knives and lights, and when the reed hut grew light, they saw Nampti sitting in the middle, and little Oukiep rubbing her arms with buchu. And they said: "Where is the lion?"

And little Oukiep was ashamed and he said: "I was afraid in the dark. I must have dreamed." And they greeted Nampti with sweet words.

And she always remained foremost among the women.

THE RAIN BULL

It is the great danger that makes the people move to the hills.

The true home is the plain, where there is much game, and where one can see far; where the spoor lies deep and stays long; where one can smell the wind and see the dust cloud at the edge of the sky.

Everyone is the enemy of the baboon. If it sets foot on the plain, everyone shouts: "There they are!" Even the children grab their small bows and arrows, and their eyes glisten, and, ducking all the while, they start walking – when the baboons come down. From every direction they are stalked; wild dog, lion, leopard, wolf, jackal – all lick their lips when they hear the words: "There they are!" Therefore, because of this great enmity, the baboons live in the mountains.

If somebody makes his dwelling there, we say in our hearts: "Great trouble has borne down on him. Now he is in the unwholesome place where the springbuck do not stay and where he looks for a spoor in vain."

High in the Langkloof the old woman Galepa made her hut, when the shelter on the plain became too narrow for her. And everyone said: "This way it is good; now she is where she belongs. Let her make her black potions there among the baboons, where she cannot harm the people with them."

But there was sadness among the young people because of the two young children, Nampti and the Hawk Wing, the daughters of her daughter whom she had killed with a spell; for they were beautiful girls, who could beat the drum and were foremost in the dance, and all the young people drew close to them when the hunters came home.

Nampti was the one who always laughed, and they called her the Heart-of-the-Daybreak.[8] And when they moved to the Langkloof, a few of the young people often went to the mountain to look for fruit.

But the old woman Galepa blocked their way and waved her arms, and she sang a magic song that made the heart grow weak:

> The little grey hawk makes her nest in the cliff;
> In vain come the werewolf and the jackal;
> In vain the red meerkat watches.
> A stone falls from the heights;
> The trail of blood leads to the plain;
> Her nest is safe.

Then they clicked with the tongue against the teeth as they turned back, and one said to the other: "The old one, Galepa, is already very old. When the wind has covered her tracks,[9] the young girls will not live alone on the mountain."

The Hawk Wing gathered food; their water hole was under the last little cliff, and every morning at the break of day Nampti went to fetch water; and long she stood on the stone ridge and looked at the plain from where she could see the smoke rising, and her heart mourned within her. She did not laugh any more; and she sang the song of yearning.

> What becomes of the girl who is always alone?
> She waits no more for the coming of the hunters;
> She makes no fire out of blackthorn.[10]
> The wind blows past her ears;
> She no longer hears the dance tune;
> The voice of the storyteller is dead.
> No-one calls her from afar
> To speak sweet words.

> She hears the voice of the wind only,
> And the wind mourns always
> Because it is lonely.

And she saw her shadow in the water, and the laughter was far from her cheeks.

One day, when she had been standing for a long time, she saw the young people with the dogs and the feather reeds,[11] for the springbuck had come. She had seen the dust of their approach a long while before. And when she looked into the water again, she saw a mist clouding her shadow in the water, and she said: "It is the tears in my eyes!" And she heard a song being sung – very softly. And she said: "It is the small child of the Wind that is singing." But her heart trembled within her body.

And it seemed as if the song was coming out of the water. And Nampti said: "The Wind knows me by name."

> The tracks of the Heart-of-the-Daybreak!
> Long had I seen them in the dew
> Before the sun burned them away;
> The little tracks of Nampti,
> That make my heart sing.

And she wondered and gazed into the water for a long time, and deep in the shadows she saw a stirring like a mountain cloud that the wind had seized; and she took fright and quickly filled her calabash with water, and ran up the kloof.

And when she told her grandmother and sister of this thing, the sister said: "You are hearing things, and you are seeing other things that are not there. It is your thinking strings."[12]

And the old woman gave her a potion to cast into the water; and she said: "Something unwholesome lives there."

And the next day Nampti went out early, and she threw the potion into the water; and there was a great stirring in the water, and before she could take fright, a young hunter stood before her on the bank, with a long bow in his hand; his arms were glinting with rings, and around his neck were many beads, like the rainbow. And he held Nampti by the kaross, and spoke sweet, very sweet words. But her blood was cold from her great fright, and she said: "How is it that you are here, and you are not of our people? The hunters are all with the springbuck, and you are on the mountain."

And he laughed at Nampti, and he said: "When you come to fetch water tomorrow, wear all your adornments."[13]

And she said: "It is not our custom to wear beads and bracelets when we work."

And when she filled the calabash, he said: "It is mine." And she walked away quickly with the calabash on her head, and from a distance she looked back, and she saw him enter the water again, and a cloud came over the waterhole, and it drifted away over the wild olive trees. And there was great wonder in the heart of Nampti.

And when she told her grandmother, the old woman said: "It is the Rain." And she taught her the greeting that she should use if he came again; and the grandmother sang a song of joy. And the Hawk Wing said: "The girl dreams while the sun is shining. Bad things will happen to her."

And when she came down the path the next morning, a few of the young hunters from the plain were near the mountain, preparing feather sticks for the springbuck, and they called to her: "When are you coming again, Nampti? Our hearts are waiting for you! The meat is plentiful, and we dance round the fires every day. Tomorrow we shall leave your meat near the water."

But she said nothing. She merely waved with her hand, for her heart was full of wonder at the Hunter-of-the-Water.

And when she came to the Rock Pool, Nampti saw him sitting on the edge, and he was gazing deep into the water; and she hid behind the wild olive, for she was shy because she was wearing beads while working. And she heard him calling softly: "Nampti, Nampti, the sun is burning your tracks away. I am waiting, I am waiting!"

And when she came out, he beckoned with his hand, and slowly he sank into the water, and she saw only the great cloud above the water. And she waited for a long time before scooping the water; but when she bent down with the calabash, she heard him say from the water: "It is mine!" And the water stirred, and a dense cloud covered everything, and she saw the Rain Bull[14] coming out of the cloud, and he knelt down before her.

And she felt her heart calling for her to climb onto his back; and she put down the calabash and climbed onto his back, and she felt him walking out of the cloud back into the water, and she closed her eyes tightly, and she felt the water around her body.

And when she felt the warmth of the sun again, she opened her eyes, and she saw that she was in a big werf with new reed huts like those of a bridegroom. And a fire was burning, and she saw the goats in the shelters, and everything in abundance. And by the great fire stood the hunter with the long bow, and he called her the way the bridegroom calls the bride.

And the next morning when the springbuck hunters brought the meat, they saw the Hawk Wing coming down the path with the calabash. And they called: "Here is the gift for Nampti!" And she said: "My sister has run away to the plain. Her tracks were last seen at the water's edge."

And they gave the meat to the Hawk Wing, and their hearts were heavy because of the disappearance of Nampti.

MARAIS'S NOTES

1. Also Sesotho. Great River Bushmen took over the word. The letters tg represent the Bushman click of the tongue.
2. Among the wild Bushmen it was a solemn greeting to sprinkle buchu under the arms. Usually it was done by a lesser person to his superior.
3. Water from a very small covered source, which is sucked through a reed and spat into eggshells.
4. A common Bushman nickname for one who is lame. The wolf walks as if he is lame in one hind leg.
5. An expression of gratitude.
6. The Pleiades, or Seven Sisters.
7. Between the rising and setting of the Seven Sisters: at the beginning of winter.
8. A well-known Bushman tale existing in many forms. In some the Heart-of-the-Daybreak is a girl, in others a man.
9. The Bushmen believe that the tracks are part of a person. When a person is buried, a wind comes up that covers all his tracks, so that nothing of him will remain behind.
10. For coals, in expectation of the meat that will be brought by the hunters.
11. Used to trap the springbuck among the hunters.
12. The Bushmen say that a person thinks and dreams and imagines by means of strings.
13. Ornaments like beads, rings, etc., that are worn only during celebrations.
14. Appears in many stories, and is often represented in paintings.

TRANSLATOR'S GLOSSARY:

Bushman/San: Although the name San has been used in the title, the name Bushman has been retained for historical purposes in Marais's introduction and notes.
Das-se-Kant: place of the das (a rock rabbit)
dwaalstorie: a wandering or wanderer's tale. The term has associations of changing as a result of retelling.
Jakkalsdraai: the place where the jackal turns
Makding: literally a tame thing
meerkat: mongoose
oribi: animal familiar
Pylstert: literally Arrow Tail
ramkie: a string instrument
Ta: father
Tonteldoos Vuurdop: literally Tinderbox Fiery Top
Tuit-Miershoop: literally pointed anthill
uintjies: the bulbs of nutsedge or nut grass
werf: farmyard, but when in the context of a nomadic group, it refers to any temporary settlement